Armond Goes to a Party
A book about Asperger's and friendship

by Nancy Carlson
and her friend Armond Isaak

Library of Congress Cataloging-in-Publication Data
Carlson, Nancy L., author.
    Armond goes to a party : a book about Asperger's and friendship / by Nancy Carlson and her friend, Armond Isaak.
        pages cm
    Audience: 5–9.
    Summary: "A boy with Asperger's overcomes his social challenges to help a friend celebrate her birthday"— Provided by publisher.
    ISBN-13: 978-1-57542-466-8 (hardback)
    ISBN-10: 1-57542-466-5 (hard cover)
    ISBN-13: 978-1-57542-467-5 (soft cover)
    ISBN-13: 978-1-57542-595-5 (ebook)
  1. Asperger's syndrome in children—Juvenile literature. 2. Autistic Children—Life skills guides—Juvenile literature. 3. Socialization—Juvenile literature.
I. Isaak, Armond, author. II. Title.
    RJ506.A9C384 2014
    618.92'858832—dc23
                                    2013050366

eBook ISBN: 978-1-57542-595-5

Reading Level Grade 2; Interest Level Ages 5–9;
Fountas & Pinnell Guided Reading Level K

Edited by Eric Braun
Cover and interior design by Tasha Kenyon

10 9 8 7 6 5 4 3 2 1
Printed in China
R18860114

Free Spirit Publishing Inc.
Minneapolis, MN
(612) 338-2068
help4kids@freespirit.com
www.freespirit.com

To Armond—
So glad you took my class at the Loft!

"It's time for Felicia's party!"
Armond's mom said.

"Armond, are you listening to me?"

"It's time for the party.
Are you ready to go?"

"I can't go to a party!" Armond said.
"I'm reading."

"You can read any time," his mom said.

"But parties make me nervous," Armond said.
"What if balloons pop?"

"And parties are disorganized.
I don't like when things are disorganized."

"What if something stinks at the party?" Armond asked. He had a very sensitive nose.

"Worst of all, I feel invisible at parties because I can't think of anything to say."

"Sometimes I feel like everyone is a branch on the same tree, and I'm the lonely stick in the yard."

"And besides," Armond said, "a party is not on my Saturday schedule. I have my basketball game, and my team needs me." Armond didn't play very much, but he always cheered for his team.

"Don't worry about basketball," his mom said.
"The party is before the game, so you won't miss it."

6

"And Felicia will feel sad if you don't help her celebrate her birthday. She's a good friend."

Armond thought about that. He wasn't sure how Felicia would feel, but he did know she would listen to him talk about dinosaurs. (Other kids usually weren't interested.) And Felicia didn't care that he had Asperger's.

"Okay, I'll go," Armond finally said. "Even though it will be really hard."

"If you need a break at the party, you can ask Felicia's mom for help," his mom said.

When Armond got to the party, balloons were everywhere. That made him nervous.

Felicia's little brother had a smelly diaper that made Armond feel sick.

11

Soon, more kids arrived.

Then *more* kids arrived.

The party got loud and disorganized.

Nobody wanted to talk about dinosaurs, and Armond couldn't think of anything else to say.

He felt nervous . . .

cranky . . .

and invisible.

When it was time for lunch . . .

Armond said, "I need a break!"

Since Felicia and her mom were Armond's good friends, they knew just what to do.

They brought him to a quiet room where he could read . . .

play Legos . . .

and think about dinosaurs.

When Armond was ready to rejoin the party, it was just in time to give Felicia her present . . .

sing "Happy Birthday" . . .

and eat a cupcake that smelled (and tasted) delicious.

When the party was over, Armond helped Felicia organize her new toys.

Soon his mom showed up to take him to basketball. "How was the party?" she asked.

"The party was hard," Armond admitted.

"I'm glad you were here, though," Felicia said.

24

Armond thought about that.
The party was fun, even though
it was hard. And he was proud
of himself. He was a good
friend. "I'm glad I was here,
too," Armond said.

A Note to Grown-Ups About Asperger's Syndrome and Friendship

Armond Isaak and Nancy Carlson teamed up to write this book so more kids and grown-ups can learn about autism spectrum disorders (ASD) and Asperger's syndrome. They want to help kids with autism or Asperger's make friends.

"Being at school can be hard," Armond says. "But not because of the schoolwork. It is hard to find friends. Sometimes I feel like no one likes me. Most of the time, I don't fit in with the other kids my age, and this makes me sad. I act younger compared to other kids my age."

Kids with autism or Asperger's often struggle to make friends. Their behavior seems out of sync with that of other kids their age, and they have difficulty reading social cues and understanding others' feelings.

You can help kids make friends and learn social skills by starting a friendship group. Invite kids with and without autism and do social skills activities such as figuring out and discussing facial expressions, telling social stories, and role-playing social situations. Keep it lighthearted by including other games.

Encourage empathy by teaching all kids about the characteristics of autism and Asperger's.

"Big parties make me feel left out," Armond says. "They are loud and noisy with kids running everywhere. I try to talk to kids but no one seems to hear me. Even with my family, I don't like big parties or lots of people around me. When we go to my Grandma and Grandpa's house, I always go downstairs to be alone. I am happy being away from all the noise."

Many kids with autism or Asperger's are uncomfortable in crowds and at parties, and it's not fair to force them to do something that's painful for them. However, sometimes being a good friend means socializing. You can help encourage kids to spend time with friends by acknowledging their feelings and providing breaks, like Felicia and her mom did in the story.

"I get upset when things don't happen as I am expecting," Armond says. "When things pop out of order, it is hard and frustrating for me."

Kids with autism or Asperger's generally thrive on routine. If you need to change a routine, give them ample notice.

"Lots of things come easy for me," says Armond, who has played lead roles in plays. "I can focus really easily, which is good when I want to memorize my lines. I love being onstage. Schoolwork also comes easily for me. I love to learn."

Many kids with autism or Asperger's are very smart. Acknowledge their strengths, whatever they are, and encourage them to develop their talents. Provide them opportunities to do the things they like to do.

About the Authors

Nancy Carlson is an accomplished children's book author and illustrator who has published more than 60 books. A lifelong Minnesotan, Nancy graduated from the Minneapolis College of Art and Design with a major in printmaking. She believes that life should be fun for everyone, but especially for children. This optimistic message permeates her picture books and provides a positive counterpoint to much of what children are influenced by in today's society. Her characters convey positive messages without being "preachy." They gently remind children what is right.

Nancy is also a guest author and illustrator at over 150 school classrooms each year and has touched the lives of thousands of children across the country. She lives in Minneapolis. Contact Nancy at **www.nancycarlson.com**.

Armond Isaak taught himself to read when he was three years old and hasn't stopped since. Besides books, his loves include Legos, playing the trumpet, and acting, and he is a proud Boy Scout. Now in middle school, Armond has been learning to embrace his uniqueness instead of fight it, and he has a small circle of friends with similar interests. He reached out to Nancy to do this book because he wants to help every young boy or girl with Asperger's realize they are not alone in a world where they often feel lonely and out of place.

Armond lives with his mom, dad, sisters Emma and Mary, cat Tigger, and dog Piper in New Hope, Minnesota.

More Great Books from Free Spirit

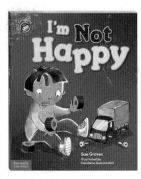

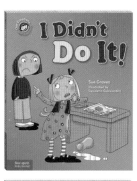

Our Emotions and Behavior Series
by Sue Graves, illustrated by Desideria Guicciardini

Small children have big feelings. The Our Emotions and Behavior series uses cheerful, brightly illustrated stories to help kids understand how their emotions and actions are related—and how they can learn to manage both. Follow along as Noah, Ben, Nora, and their friends discover ways to deal with anger, fears, rules, sharing, and more. At the end of each book, a two-page series of pictures invites kids to tell a story in their own words. A special section for adults suggests discussion questions and ideas for guiding children to talk about their feelings.

28 pp., illust., 4-color, H/C, 7¾" x 9½". Ages 4–8.

This Morning Sam Went to Mars
by Nancy Carlson

Sam is always daydreaming about exploring space and the deepest seas, which is awesome—except when he's supposed to be focusing on schoolwork or stuff at home. It seems like all he hears is, "Focus, Sam!" and "Pay attention!" The doctor says Sam is lucky: He has a very powerful brain! But he does need some help focusing. She gives Sam and his dad lots of strategies to try to improve focus, like staying organized, eating better food, and asking for help when he needs it. Sam's favorite strategy? Make time for imagination!

32 pp., illust., 4-color, H/C & S/C, 11¼" x 9¼". Ages 4–8.

Zach Rules Series
by William Mulcahy, illustrated by Darren McKee

Zach, his brothers Alex and Scott, and his parents are a typical family. The boys struggle with getting along, frustrations, social issues, and other everyday problems typical with kids ages 5 to 8. Each book in the Zach Rules series presents a single, simple storyline involving one such problem. As each story develops, Zach and readers learn straightforward tools for coping with their struggles. The tools are presented graphically to make them easier to understand and remember. Each book concludes with a short note to adults to help parents, teachers, counselors, and other grown-ups reinforce the books' messages and practice the skills with their kids.

32 pp., illust., 4-color, H/C, 8" x 8". Ages 5–8.

Interested in purchasing multiple quantities and receiving volume discounts?
Contact edsales@freespirit.com or call 1.800.735.7323 and ask for Education Sales.

Many Free Spirit authors are available for speaking engagements, workshops, and keynotes.
Contact speakers@freespirit.com or call 1.800.735.7323.

For pricing information, to place an order, or to request a free catalog, contact:

free spirit PUBLISHING®

217 Fifth Avenue North • Suite 200 • Minneapolis, MN 55401-1299
toll-free 800.735.7323 • local 612.338.2068 • fax 612.337.5050
help4kids@freespirit.com • www.freespirit.com